… Great Artists

Paul Gauguin

Adam G. Klein

ABDO
Publishing Company

**visit us at
www.abdopublishing.com**

Published by ABDO Publishing Company, 4940 Viking Drive, Edina, Minnesota 55435. Copyright © 2007 by Abdo Consulting Group, Inc. International copyrights reserved in all countries. No part of this book may be reproduced in any form without written permission from the publisher. The Checkerboard Library™ is a trademark and logo of ABDO Publishing Company.

Printed in the United States.

Cover Photo: Bridgeman Art Library
Interior Photos: Art Resource pp. 1, 9, 13, 15, 17, 21, 23, 25, 27; Bridgeman Art Library pp. 4, 5, 11, 19, 28; Corbis p. 29

Series Coordinator: Megan M. Gunderson
Editors: Heidi M. Dahmes, Megan M. Gunderson
Cover Design: Neil Klinepier
Interior Design: Dave Bullen

Library of Congress Cataloging-in-Publication Data

Klein, Adam G., 1976-
  Paul Gauguin / Adam G. Klein.
    p. cm. -- (Great artists)
  Includes index.
  ISBN-10 1-59679-729-0
  ISBN-13 978-1-59679-729-1
  1. Gauguin, Paul, 1848-1903--Juvenile literature. 2. Painters--France--Biography--Juvenile literature. I. Gauguin, Paul, 1848-1903. II. Title III. Series: Klein, Adam G., 1976- . Great artists.

ND553.G27K54 2006
759.4--dc22

2005017887

Contents

Paul Gauguin 4
Timeline 6
Fun Facts 7
Young Traveler 8
The Navy 10
Starting Over 12
Changing Times 14
Copenhagen 16
The Next New Thing 18
Paradise 20
Van Gogh 22
More Synthetism 24
Tahiti 26
A New Cause 28
Glossary 30
Saying It 31
Web Sites 31
Index 32

Paul Gauguin

Paul Gauguin experienced all sides of life. He was rich and poor, healthy and ill, a success and a failure. Gauguin was a world traveler, and he never tired of trying new things. Eventually, his journeys led him to some of the world's most remote places.

As an artist, Gauguin learned from the **Impressionist** movement. But later, he rejected Impressionism. Instead, he became one of the most important Postimpressionists. He also helped create Synthetism. This art movement focused on the synthesis, or combination, of both objects and feelings in a piece of art.

Gauguin became famous for painting the people and the bright colors of Tahiti.

Gauguin created paintings, drawings, and pottery. He experimented with the styles of other artists. Then, he used what he learned from their work to create his own style. Through his artwork, Gauguin influenced and inspired many artists who followed him.

Gauguin painted several self-portraits. He used a mirror to paint himself. So in this work, the painting in the background is backward.

Timeline

1848 ~ On June 7, Eugène-Henri-Paul Gauguin was born in Paris, France.

1865 ~ Gauguin joined the merchant marine.

1872 ~ Gauguin and Émile Schuffenecker began visiting galleries and creating paintings; Gauguin met Mette Sophie Gad.

1873 ~ Gauguin married Gad.

1876 ~ The Salon accepted *Landscape at Viroflay*.

1880 to 1882 ~ Gauguin participated in Impressionist exhibitions.

1886 ~ Gauguin participated in the last group Impressionist exhibition; Gauguin painted *Four Breton Women*.

1887 ~ Gauguin completed *Among the Mangoes* and *By the Sea*.

1888 ~ Gauguin produced *Vision After the Sermon*.

1889 ~ Gauguin painted *The Yellow Christ* and *The Green Christ*.

1897 ~ Gauguin painted *Where Do We Come From? What Are We? Where Are We Going?*

1903 ~ On May 8, Gauguin died on the island of Hiva Oa.

- While working at Bertin, Paul Gauguin spent his lunch breaks visiting galleries and his evenings drawing.

- In 1888, Vincent van Gogh suggested that several artists exchange paintings. Gauguin, Van Gogh, Charles Laval, and Émile Bernard each painted a self-portrait to trade.

- Gauguin had a distinctive wardrobe. Because of his time in Pont-Aven, Gauguin sometimes wore a traditional Breton vest. And after seeing Buffalo Bill Cody's Wild West Show, he bought himself a cowboy hat.

- Today, a museum in Mataiea, Tahiti, allows visitors to learn about Gauguin's island life and work.

Young Traveler

Eugène-Henri-Paul Gauguin was born on June 7, 1848, in Paris, France. His mother, Aline Chazal, was the daughter of the famous writer Flora Tristan. Paul's father, Clovis Gauguin, was a journalist. Paul was the second child in the Gauguin family. His sister, Marie, had been born a year earlier.

During the mid-1800s, France was becoming increasingly dangerous. Louis-Napoléon was elected president and eventually became Emperor Napoléon III. Clovis did not favor the new government, so the Gauguin family decided to leave France.

In 1851, the family set sail for Lima, Peru. The journey was long and difficult, and Clovis died along the way. In Peru, Aline's wealthy relatives took in the family. Conditions were poor in Lima, but Paul enjoyed many privileges. Eventually, the government in Peru was also overthrown. So in 1855, the Gauguins returned to France.

At Aline's suggestion, Gauguin tried woodcarving on the voyage back to France. None of his early works remain. However, he later returned to this art form. He created *Idol with a Shell* in late 1892.

The Navy

Upon their return to France, Paul, Marie, and Aline moved to Orléans. Having grown up in Peru, Paul spoke only Spanish. But, he quickly learned French. At age 11, he began attending a school just four miles (6 km) away from Orléans. There, Paul lived in a dormitory and received his first instruction in drawing.

As a teenager, Paul decided to become a sailor. His family wanted him to join the Naval Academy so that he could become an officer. But, Paul's schoolwork was so poor that he was not allowed to take the academy's entrance exams.

Paul did not want to give up his dream of becoming a sailor. So, he joined the **merchant marine**. On December 7, 1865, Paul left from Le Havre, France.

In 1868, Paul **enlisted** in the French navy. While in the navy, he fought in the **Franco-Prussian War**. When the French lost, Paul returned home.

Gauguin spent six years sailing all over the world. It was an adventurous lifestyle, but it was also difficult.

Starting Over

Gauguin's mother had died while he was at sea. Aline had been living in Saint-Cloud, France. When Gauguin returned from the war, he found the family home destroyed.

Gauguin had lost everything he owned, including **artifacts** from Peru. At age 23, he had to start all over. A family friend named Gustave Arosa generously provided assistance. Arosa helped Gauguin get a job at the Bertin **stockbroking** firm in Paris. It was a good job, and Gauguin became wealthy.

Arosa also helped spark Gauguin's interest in art. Arosa had a large art collection, and he introduced Gauguin to many art **critics**. This exposed Gauguin to the latest thinking in the art world.

In 1872, Gauguin became friends with a coworker named Émile Schuffenecker. Schuffenecker had studied art. In their free time, the two painted together or visited galleries. Schuffenecker was a positive influence on Gauguin. He showed Gauguin that working a regular job provided the money to be an artist in his spare time.

Later in life, Gauguin painted *The Schuffenecker Family*. The portrait is not very flattering. It shows Schuffenecker distant from his family, wringing his hands.

Gauguin was also influenced by a young Danish woman named Mette Sophie Gad. Gauguin found her strength and independence attractive. The couple married in 1873 and later had five children together.

Changing Times

Since the 1600s, an institution in France called the Salon had exhibited works of art. The Salon jury only accepted traditional themes and paintings. However, the **Impressionist** movement was growing and moving away from traditional art. Impressionists wanted to create something new. This made the 1870s a very exciting time for art.

The Salon rejected many Impressionist works. So, the Impressionists began holding their own shows. Arosa supported their first exhibition in 1874.

In the mid-1870s, Gauguin met Impressionist Camille Pissarro. They became friends, and Pissarro helped Gauguin develop his art. Pissarro also introduced Gauguin to other Impressionist artists such as Claude Monet, Pierre-Auguste Renoir, Edgar Degas, and Paul Cézanne.

Breaking the Rules

Gauguin was known for copying the styles of other artists. But, he was also known for creating his own interpretations of their styles. In Flowers, Still Life (right), Gauguin used the short brushstrokes commonly found in Impressionist paintings. And the main object in the painting, the bouquet of flowers, is off center. This was something Impressionist painter Edgar Degas had done in his works.

However, Gauguin went against the normal rules of painting. In portraits, painters commonly placed people in the foreground. Gauguin bravely placed the people in the background of Flowers, Still Life. In this way, he combined a portrait and a still life in one painting, providing his interpretation of those two styles.

Gauguin experimented with **Impressionism**. Yet in 1876, his more traditional painting *Landscape at Viroflay* was accepted at the Salon. Then from 1880 to 1882, Gauguin displayed his work at Impressionist exhibitions. He also bought many Impressionist paintings. Gauguin owned several by Cézanne so that he could study that artist's work.

Copenhagen

In 1883, the French **stock** market crashed. Soon after, Gauguin lost his job at the stockbroking firm. Gauguin was happy that this would allow him to paint all the time. But in order to survive, Gauguin and his family moved to Copenhagen, Denmark. Mette's family was still there and Paul hoped they would help support his family.

In Copenhagen, Gauguin got a job as a salesman. But, he could not speak Danish. So, he did not enjoy much success. And, his wife's family did not approve of him. The situation was stressful, and Gauguin felt lost.

Eventually, the strain on Gauguin's marriage was too much. So, he took his son Clovis and returned to Paris in 1885. Gauguin hoped that one day his family would be reunited.

Back in Paris, Gauguin and Clovis lived in various places. Schuffenecker supported them a little, but conditions were not good. At one point, Gauguin and Clovis lived off of little more than boiled rice. Eventually, Clovis entered a boarding school and Gauguin began preparing to exhibit his artwork.

In Copenhagen, Gauguin struggled to find work and support his family. Despite the hardships, he still found comfort in painting. He painted *Skaters in the Park of Frederiksberg* in 1884.

The Next New Thing

The **Impressionists** held their last group exhibition in 1886. Gauguin, Pissarro, and others were joined by newer artists such as Georges Seurat. Seurat was trying a new **technique** called **Pointillism**. So, Gauguin's works did not receive much attention. Impressionism was coming to an end.

Gauguin wanted to try another art form. So, he experimented with **ceramics**. Gauguin had been interested in pottery since his time in Peru. But, he had never tried to create it.

Eventually, his search for a new art form brought Gauguin to Pont-Aven, France. Many artists traveled to this village in the Brittany region. There, Gauguin painted the local people, especially the women.

When he returned to Paris at the end of 1886, Gauguin painted *Four Breton Women*. His work was moving away from Impressionism, but he was still looking for a new style.

Gauguin never stayed long in any one place. And, he was looking for something more **exotic**. So, Gauguin decided to leave

Four Breton Women represents Gauguin's changing style. The short brushstrokes and attention to light reflect the Impressionist movement. His move toward Postimpressionism shows in the use of bold outlines.

France and find work near the **Panama Canal**. Charles Laval, a friend he met in Pont-Aven, decided to join him. On April 10, 1887, the two left France for Panama.

Paradise

Gauguin hoped that Panama would be an **exotic** place to work. But when the men arrived, they were discouraged. Poverty was widespread. Both Gauguin and Laval caught tropical diseases. And, they were unable to find acceptable employment.

So, Gauguin and Laval decided to move on. They raised enough money to get on a boat heading to the island of Martinique. When they arrived in June 1887, they finally found the paradise they were looking for.

On Martinique, Gauguin painted landscapes as well as the daily life of the islanders. *Among the Mangoes* and *By the Sea* display Gauguin's talent for capturing Martinique.

Meanwhile, someone in France bought some of Gauguin's pottery. Schuffenecker sent him the money, and Gauguin bought

In *By the Sea*, Gauguin experimented with painting bold lines of color. Scholars believe Gauguin's Martinique paintings indicate his break from Impressionism.

a ticket back to France in 1887. Gauguin took a few paintings with him. But more important, he returned with the bright colors that would later define his style.

Van Gogh

By November 1887, Gauguin was back in Paris and living with Schuffenecker. Gauguin eventually came in contact with artists Émile Bernard and Vincent van Gogh. Van Gogh's brother, Theo, began buying Gauguin's pottery and paintings.

In 1888, Gauguin moved back to Pont-Aven, where he was joined by Bernard. There, the two discussed and traded ideas about art. Gauguin and Bernard decided to base their new paintings on both real and imaginary things. Together, they helped form the Synthetist movement. *Vision After the Sermon* is one of Gauguin's first Synthetist works.

The same year, Van Gogh set up a new studio in Arles, France. He wanted to create a place for artists to gather and share ideas. Gauguin knew about Van Gogh's new studio. He was reluctant to join Van Gogh. But eventually, Theo convinced Gauguin to give it a try. Gauguin arrived in Arles on October 23, 1888.

Artist's Corner

Gauguin studied the works of other artists before developing his own style. So, he is associated with several different art movements. These include Impressionism, Postimpressionism, Symbolism, and Synthetism.

Impressionists painted by directly observing things. The Postimpressionists expanded on this idea. Gauguin painted things he observed, but he didn't paint them as realistically. He became more concerned with colors and shapes. He was especially inspired by the blocks of color and bold outlines used in stained glass.

Gauguin also helped develop Synthetist art. This style emphasized the combination of shapes and feelings in a work. Gauguin also combined real and imaginary elements in his Synthetist pieces. In *Vision After the Sermon (right)*, Gauguin painted Breton women praying after a sermon. But, he didn't just show someone delivering the sermon in the background. Instead, he painted what the listeners might imagine after hearing the story.

More Synthetism

Gauguin and Van Gogh were not suited to live together. Van Gogh tried to get Gauguin to stay in Arles. But problems multiplied, and the two artists got in an argument. On December 24, 1888, Van Gogh cut off part of his own ear and was hospitalized.

Gauguin left for Paris the next day. In May 1889, he visited the Paris International Exposition. It renewed Gauguin's interest in the **exotic**. He saw displays of artwork and **culture** from countries in Asia and islands of the Pacific Ocean. Soon, Gauguin decided to travel again.

First, Gauguin returned to Pont-Aven. There, he created more paintings based on Synthetism. These included *The Yellow Christ* and *The Green Christ*. He also spent time in nearby Le Pouldu.

In November 1890, Gauguin returned to Paris. He sold some paintings at an auction in 1891. Gauguin used the money for a voyage to Tahiti.

Several of Gauguin's works had religious themes. He painted *The Yellow Christ (inset)* in 1889. Less than a year later, Gauguin painted *Self-Portrait with Yellow Christ.*

Tahiti

Before he left for Tahiti, Gauguin visited his family in Denmark. It was the last time he would see his wife and children. In March, Gauguin's friends held a farewell banquet for him in Paris. Then, he left France.

Gauguin arrived in Papeete, Tahiti, on June 19, 1891. Tahiti was a colony, so Papeete was run by the French government. Gauguin did not travel to the other side of the world to live in European society. So, he went to Mataiea on the opposite side of the island. He hoped this area would be more **exotic**.

Mataiea's Tahitians accepted Gauguin. And, they allowed him to paint them. Gauguin painted *The Meal* in 1891. It features three Tahitian children.

Gauguin began having health problems, so he returned to Papeete. By this time, he was also running out of money. In June

In *The Meal*, Gauguin once again combined a still life and a portrait in a single work.

1893, Gauguin left Tahiti to return to France. He brought with him 66 paintings and several sculptures. Gauguin had already sent some of his work back to France.

A New Cause

On August 30, 1893, Gauguin arrived in France. There, he assembled writings and artwork into a book called *Noa Noa*. Gauguin hoped the book would educate people about his time on the island. Before the book was finished, Gauguin decided to return to Tahiti, this time for good.

Gauguin arrived back in Papeete in September 1895. He continued to paint the Tahitians, but his health was failing. Gauguin declined further after he received news that his daughter, Aline, had died. In 1897, he decided to paint a final masterpiece, *Where Do We Come From? What Are We? Where Are We Going?*

Gauguin wrote *Noa Noa* using notes he had made during his time in Tahiti.

While he was in Tahiti, Gauguin's work gained support in Paris. In late 1898, Gauguin was the talk of the Paris art world! But in 1901, he further removed himself from society. He relocated to the island of Hiva Oa. Gauguin died there on May 8, 1903.

Gauguin never stopped experimenting. His attitudes about art were an inspiration to others. His use of bright colors and his ideas about Synthetism influenced the next generation of artists. Today, Gauguin's artwork is found in museums across the world.

Gauguin is buried in Atuona, which is the main village on Hiva Oa.

Glossary

artifact - a useful object made by human skill a long time ago.
ceramic - of or relating to a nonmetallic product, such as pottery or porcelain.
critic - a professional who gives his or her opinion on art or performances.
culture - the customs, arts, and tools of a nation or people at a certain time.
enlist - to join the armed forces.
exotic - something new and different, often from a faraway place.
Franco-Prussian War - from 1870 to 1871. A war fought between France and Prussia, a former kingdom now in Germany. Prussia won the war and created the German Empire.
Impressionism - an art movement developed by French painters in the late 1800s. They depicted the natural appearances of objects by using strokes or dabs of primary colors.
merchant marine - the ships a country uses in business and the people who operate those ships.
Panama Canal - a human-made, narrow canal across Panama that connects the Atlantic and Pacific oceans.
Pointillism - the use of small brushstrokes and small dots of color so that they blend together when seen from a distance.
stock - money that represents part of a business. People who purchase stock can own part of the company. A stockbroking firm is a company that buys and sells stock for others.
technique - a method or style in which something is done.

Camille Pissarro - kaw-meey pee-saw-roh
Georges Seurat - zhawrzh soo-raw
Hiva Oa - hee-vuh OH-uh
Le Havre - luh HAHVRUH
Orléans - awr-lay-AHN
Papeete - pah-pay-AY-tay
Paul Cézanne - pawl say-zawn

To learn more about Paul Gauguin, visit ABDO Publishing Company on the World Wide Web at **www.abdopublishing.com**. Web sites about Gauguin are featured on our Book Links page. These links are routinely monitored and updated to provide the most current information available.

Index

A
Among the Mangoes 20
Arosa, Gustave 12, 14
B
Bernard, Émile 22
By the Sea 20
C
Cézanne, Paul 14, 15
D
Degas, Edgar 14
Denmark 13, 16, 26
E
education 10
exhibitions 15, 18, 24
F
family 8, 10, 12, 13, 16, 17, 26, 28
Four Breton Women 18
Franco-Prussian War 10, 12
G
Green Christ, The 24
H
health 4, 20, 26, 28
Hiva Oa 29

I
Impressionism 4, 14, 15, 18
L
Landscape at Viroflay 15
Laval, Charles 19, 20
M
Martinique 20
Meal, The 26
Monet, Claude 14
N
Napoléon III (emperor) 8
Noa Noa (book) 28
P
Pacific Ocean 24
Panama 19, 20
Paris International Exposition 24
Peru 8, 10, 12, 18
Pissarro, Camille 14, 18
Pointillism 18
Postimpressionism 4
R
Renoir, Pierre-Auguste 14

S
Salon 14, 15
Schuffenecker, Émile 12, 17, 20, 22
Seurat, Georges 18
Synthetism 4, 22, 24, 29
T
Tahiti 24, 26, 27, 28, 29
V
van Gogh, Theo 22
van Gogh, Vincent 22, 24
Vision After the Sermon 22
W
Where Do We Come From? What Are We? Where Are We Going? 28
Y
Yellow Christ, The 24